THE DOG SEATED NEXT TO ME

by

MEG POKRASS

Pelekinesis

The Dog Seated Next to Me by Meg Pokrass

ISBN: 978-1-949790-23-8

eISBN: 978-1-949790-24-5

Library of Congress Control Number: 2019945697

Layout and book design by Mark Givens

Cover art: "Blue Dog" by Cooper Renner, 2019

Author photo by Miriam Berkeley

First Pelekinesis Printing 2019

For information: Pelekinesis, 112 Harvard Ave #65, Claremont, CA 91711 USA

www.pelekinesis.com

THE DOG SEATED NEXT TO ME

by

MEG POKRASS

PRAISE FOR MEG POKRASS

"The people in these stories need Meg Pokrass. Their lives are tough but her imagination is the fire-lasso that can save them, save us. In her work, off-kilter is the same as clear-eyed focus. Here, strange and normal go hand-in-hand, a marriage that explains nothing but makes so much clear. Time after time, these little stories read big."

—Bob Hicok

"The nuanced tonal complexity, which can go from the whimsical to a darker irony in the turn of a phrase, has been a signature feature of the work of Meg Pokrass. That complexity is, in her collection, *Alligators at Night*, heightened further by the fertile invention and unpredictable interplay of these beautifully crafted pieces."

—Stuart Dybek, author of *Ecstatic Cahoots*

"The stories of Meg Pokrass are like beautiful bruises. I read them and ache. Sparse, poetic, insightful, and always astonishing. This is writing that makes you feel alive."

—Angela Readman, author of *Something Like Breathing*

"Meg Pokrass bops and slams through these little stories like some genius extraterrestrial psychic on a world tour of the human heart. Her language is supercharged and witty, with humor and sadness in approximately equal amounts."

—Bobbie Ann Mason, author of *Shiloh and Other Stories*, *In Country*, and *The Girl in the Blue Beret*

"To enter the portals of Pokrassland is to go on a magical journey: here there are sex-charged buffalo men and melancholic women who fear six-foot spiders and fall in love with their therapists. It's a place where people make bald statements and odd connections, where there are strange animals, purple stars and 'a deep-ruby moon'."

—Nuala O'Connor, author of *Joyride to Jupiter* and *Becoming Belle*

"In the universe of Meg Pokrass's fictions, planets are gloriously misaligned, stars and suns trail love and desperate sadness, black holes serve up dogs, spiders, cats, and galaxies explode everything we thought we knew about the human heart. It is an ever-expanding universe. No other like it."

—Pamela Painter, author of *Wouldn't You Like to Know*

For Miles, Hannah and Sian

CONTENTS

"Even in Siberia there is happiness."
Anton Chekhov

A DETACHED KIND OF IMAGINARY CRUELTY

THERE is a flustered buffalo in a hotel bed, and it is a man, and it is a man who wants me so much he is levitating like an endangered animal. He is mastering the art of being made extinct. I am that kind of pony, here today, gone tomorrow, all fancy and prancing and cruel. I administer pleasure, and then disappear, because I can, because I am a splinter, that is all I am when not making an animal happy.

There are the ones to take inside and to rock like babies, to rock until they groan and ask for pancakes.

There are ways to fly up against the heat of a man's sex, to singe his wings because nothing lasts longer than a good beer, or a fingerling potato on a cold night.

FIRE EATER

SHE had not made love with him for a year and she didn't know why. She would start to count the days, and then she'd stop. She'd get caught on a number, seventy-five, and feel as if she were trapped in an elevator. She believed they would talk and they would come to some understanding, clang back together. She would train herself to be reassured. She'd roll back to sleep knowing, until the dreams came.

In dreams she was kissing the other one, the one she had not yet met. She could feel his eyebrows, could reach out and touch his shirt. She'd recall his way of writing things to her in a semi-serious way, as if none of it really mattered. Their love would die, too. All would end.

She'd lie in bed like a fire-eater in the morning, arguing with herself, and waiting for her husband to return. She told herself that if he opened the front door again, walked back in just one more time—things would feel better.

SPIDER

THERE'S a spider in the bathroom, I tell him. It's six feet tall, I say. I wake him up and tell him to save me. I pee a few times a night and can't imagine slipping into the cold bathroom alone, facing this spider head-on. It's frigid here in Siberia. Outside, nothing can live for long. We humans and insects are all in the same boat, hoping for food, praying for love. Some people wander out and let the cold take care of their problems, let the cold win. Please, take care of Mr. Creepy, I say. My husband goes into the bathroom in his bare feet, hands in the air. He stands there, letting the spider crawl right up his leg, right up to his face. His skin is warm, the spider is happy. His legs are so long, perfect runways. They used to make me feel safe. "This cute little dot?" my husband says. He says this to me about our spider problem. He calls it a dot. "How would you feel if you were trapped in someone else's life?" he says.

SAAB STORY

"WHAT are the chances of getting hit by a meteorite?" We were at Point Reyes seashore, had driven hours north of the city to watch the sunset. We drove to beautiful places in our untrustworthy car, wondering where and when it would die. "We live in the world's most perfect place," he'd remind me. "Except for earthquakes."

I wanted him to have a theory. To explain things to me. To me, our lives were worrisome, driving away from an apartment filled with unpaid bills to see another perfect sunset.

"I don't know anything about the statistical risk of death by meteorite," my husband said.

The Saab sounded asthmatic—creaky, loud. I thought about the man who sold it to us. Bruce. He told us that he used to sell timeshares before he sold cars.

'This car suits the two of you," he said.

His lips seemed to collapse on each other as he moved his mouth around. He was out of breath, fanning his face with a marketing flier. There was pressure on him to sell us a car, pressure on us to buy the cheapest car we could still feel safe in.

We parked by the sea. The sunset was so orange and exotic, a blanket of fluffy sky. We perched in our heated lemon, staring at the glow.

PANCAKES AND EGGS

STEPPING off the train from L.A, bloated with being real, Sam squinted at me as if looking directly into the sun. His fingernails were woman-nice, his mustache well-combed and his gray curls stiff with man-gel. Like a poster for a gentleman—supercilious now that I look back, but not then. Just that sweet smile, black wool scarf, dapper when he stepped off the train.

"I'm hungry for pancakes or eggs," Sam said. "And I bet you know where to get them."

I was a "dish," he said, with my own "funk-style" pockets and dumb-pocket jeans and dyke-ish hat.

"You are a silly goof. This is what nobody knows about you."

"Gosh, thanks."

He smiled.

THE SEASON OF CHEER

ANALYSIS was going well. The doctor brought in a box of thin mints. She stopped talking about her feelings, and they just sat there, sharing them. He turned on the radio, Bach's Brandenburg Concertos. She used to complain December exhausted her. Now she looked forward to the Christmas lights going up in and around the doctor's office building.

Instead of asking about her appetite, the doctor suggested he buy her a soft violet colored scarf, one he saw in a window somewhere. He said he'd thought of her, that he was sure it would bring out her colors. Her smile. The valley of good cheer was just around the corner. The way she loved him, had begun to love him: a December feeling. Short bright days, long dark nights, listening to Bach and thinking about her doctor.

UNCLE SHUG'S

AT Uncle Shug's, we're in love with each other again. Laughing, loving each other's faces. We're the funny kids nobody ever wants to be away from, like siblings, but with sex. He's me and I'm him. I sit on his lap, and he doesn't look around to see if his mother is watching, making him feel too guilty to breathe. Here in Uncle Shug's we're sharing key lime pie, and I'm feeling his warm fine skin, and I'm kissing the places where his golden hair used to be. He's calling me 'Vixen of the Outer Sunset', kissing my lips the way he did before his mother's car accident, before he curled up inside himself after I was mugged.

We order Cokes. Remember these sugary cravings? I say, pretty sure I'm dreaming this whole thing up. We're divorced now, right?

That's okay, he says. I'm digging this dream, how we're in it together, the way we were in the beginning. Don't smother it with too much thinking, vixen.

Under the table, our feet find each other. I wiggle my toes beneath his fine, fungal nails.

What's next? I say. I'm covered with glaze, just like the honey-baked ham he used to slice up on Christmas morning. Here we are, boneless. Here we are, young and funny and in love with the world. Here we are, waiting till the hand-cut potatoes arrive.

CARTOONS

HE wouldn't listen. Never obeyed. He didn't want to do what she wanted him to do. She stopped asking and moved her hips to the sound of his heart.

Thump. Thump.

Ten minutes of this.

Take it out, she said. He did not want to hear this, but he took it out.

Now what? he asked.

Cartoons, she said. Put cartoons on, please.

MARGARET THATCHER

THE kinds of things he says about his wife. The way he describes her smile.

"Do you know who she reminds me of the most?"

"Nope, who," I say.

"She reminds me of Margaret Thatcher, the Meryl Streep one," he says. He laughs. I laugh. We laugh and sometimes I cry. He holds me and asks me what time my therapy is. "I'll walk you there on my way to the subway," he says.

The industrial veil she wore in their wedding. The school-boyish way he lifted it to kiss her. You see it in your mind like reruns of Cagney and Lacey. You like the show but it bores you and you wonder why you're lonely enough to watch it again tonight. She is the kind of woman who believes in doing things the right way the first time around. "Where did you go on your honeymoon?" you ask. "Wrong question," he says. "The real question is, would I do it again?"

I climb him and from the top of his body

I look down on his life from above. His nose like a landing pad, fleshy and strong. I see him with the wife in amusing family squeezes, imagining his nose next to his never-naked wife. I see them sharing meals, smiling with no echo, him setting a timer while she finishes her lamb.

How you amuse yourself. You talk to your therapist about all of the guys you've loved. You charm her, a weekly comedy act. You make her care about you. Even though she doesn't say it. Even though she raises her fee again because her office rent is going up.

The pitch of your lovers voice reminds you of someone. You can't remember who. "Does your wife have a nice singing voice?" you ask him. "You must be kidding," he says. He thinks you're so funny.. You imagine Margaret Thatcher in a Broadway musical. She's playing a sad, lonely person who used to have love in her life. Her hair flattens around her face, a face that used to be knowable. Her blank eyes stare at the orchestra pit.

FIXING IT UP

SHE was fixing the doctor up. Like the Beatles song, the doctor had a hole where the rain got in and kept his mind from stuff it wanted to do. For a few hours, she could take care of that.

He complimented her nightshirt.

"Kimono," she corrected.

He told her to stop wandering around the world, in circles like that, to stop pacing the floor, to come over to him, and to kneel by the bed where he sat. Rain was coming down outside some window, if not this one. A window somewhere held back hard strong rain... She began to make love by thinking of the shape of rain.

MR. SHAKY

WHEN I walked into the coffee shop, there was Mr. Shaky. I had dated him once a few months earlier and had not heard from him since.

He waved at me, a trembly little motion of the fingers. I waved back. Hello there, Mr. Shaky. How's it going?

I was there to meet my date of the week. Monty. At least he said his name was Monty. But he signed off with "Quentin." His text said: "From Monty: Let's meet for Java, kid! What do ewe say? I'm belligerent and proud of it! Tap 'er light! Quentin."

Seeing Mr. Shaky reminded me of our own date a few months ago, how he showed up wearing royal blue shorts and shower sandals. Pet rat on his shoulder. His lips trembled when he said hello. He introduced me to his friend.

"This is Rosie Rat," he said. "She's got the snuffles, so I have her on antibiotics."

Rosie had round ears. Way too cute to be a rat, so I pushed my lips into a smile. Rosie's fur reminded me of my mother's final hair color, a cross between blue and gray. She had died

MEG POKRASS

years ago, but I missed her every day.

Our date ended shortly after it began, Mr. Shaky spilling his coffee on my skirt and me telling him that I had to run home and squirt it with stain remover.

So here I was, wondering why Rosie was not on his shoulder, wondering if she might have died, when my new date sauntered in.

I noticed the hump of night-hair, like he'd slept on one side. A haystack of blond hair, dented and precariously placed. It reminded me of volunteering on an organic farm as a college student, hoping the hay wouldn't topple in the wind.

He wore a bombastic t-shirt: "tap-er-light." I tried to imagine what that meant.

Quiet as a rodent I watched him from the corner of my eye, a few customers behind me in line, peering around, probably worried I had stood him up.

I don't look anything like my profile photo. I took it with my arm extended high above my face. It white-washed all of my wrinkles out, made me look thirty years younger, like a woman who had never been divorced and had not lost her mother. Like a woman who could love a rat.

THE CAPACITY TO LOVE

CATS have the capacity to love, but they're self-sufficient. Right? So I asked Sam if he would like to get a cat, sort of like getting a family in stages. "A cat's a good starter-animal," I said. I was fishing, hoping for a sign. I wasn't getting any. Sam sat in the checkered chair, pulling skin off his foot. Thinking. He'd started pulling at various parts of his body or biting his nails. Living with me.

"Anyway," I said, "the atmosphere in this place is a bit stale, a bit tired." He looked at me for a second. My legs felt like jello, as if I might fall, as if I'd been running a race my whole life for this moment, and now my muscles were clenching up.

"Maybe we could start with an ant farm," he said. I almost laughed. I had just noticed that he resembled a large ant, his head larger than human heads were supposed to be. He couldn't find any hats that fit.

"Come over here, Monkey," he said, hooking

me by the waist. He stuck me with a kiss. His lips on my neck made a popping sound, like a suction cup. I let him keep me close, and we sat together like one load-bearing creature. He was no longer pulling at himself. He was touching me instead.

CURED

HE tasted like a bologna sandwich. And it was not his breath. It felt like a taste that lived deep inside his body. She imagined he was still grieving. His young wife had died. This kind of sadness could turn a man's mouth into some kind of pickled meat.

They were meeting again, for the fourth time, at the coffee place. She with velvet socks, which made her feel lovable. This was something he couldn't know, wouldn't care to. How she wore velvet foot coverings. Little things like this. His brain couldn't yet digest much of her wonderfulness.

The cured meat flavor theory made sense in the natural world. Tears were made of water and salt. Grief was not angular, it was soft, droopy, wet. One could soak in a pond full of it.

Humans, like amphibious animals, developed ugly traits to protect themselves. Some freaky African toad squirted blood from its eyes to offer, like a food sample, to predatory birds. This toad's blood tasted so bad, the birds flew the fuck home.

He was a Harlequin Toad to her, that kind of rare, beautiful creature, highly endangered. As time crept by, she wanted to marry him to her, take care of him, and hold him in the crook of her arm (where her cat slept, now) after diving in and out of the deep swamp of sex.

When they kissed, she felt swell-preserved and lovely. Maybe this was the cured meat talking. Salted, which meant it would never expire. She thought about asking if he'd let her pour salad dressing on his tongue, but she'd never really ask him this, he was dealing with enough.

She had always taken pride in being a messy lover, uninhibited. But here she was in love with a man who could not laugh, and she was going out of her mind. She felt like a spider, or a monkey, or a toad. She just so wanted to soap him up, get down to things.

Tired and hungry, she pulled on a mask of gentility and moderation. For the first time, after the first few martinis, she made an aggressive suggestion. "Hey, I'd like to head over to the Blue Towel. Wanna come?"

"Blue Towel, you say?"

"Yep, that's the place."

He followed her with no resistance. Seemed ready for something.

They staggered to her car. She took a group of dogs to the beach every day, so she had a blue dog towel in the back seat. It was an embarrassing towel. She washed it but not often.

"It smells like dogs in here," she said.

"Yes, it does."

He sneezed and sneezed. She pulled off one of her velvet socks and handed it to him, asked him to pet it, to feel it, smell it. He didn't register surprise. His face looked stretchy and sad. He had been sterilized by grief, and this needed to be undone.

MOUSE WOMAN

SHE and Sam stayed in different parts of their long row house now, routinely. Sam, she knew, spoke with a woman on a chat site.

Dark hair in the bathroom sink, curled up, all at-once back together in a drain-clogging knot, made her think about the last time she washed a champagne glass carefully by hand, and still Sam told her it appeared unclean. Why was his hair in the sink now tangled with hers?

Sam cries, but not often. She hates to see him cry.

And she wishes she had never commented on Sam's music in the living room. It sounded funereal, all of the time. It may have been wrong of her to object, but she did not want to hear this music anymore, it had been long enough, and she did not like the canned, scripted words from Sam's mouth to her ears.

* * *

Sam was in love. She had never known him happy like this. He sang new songs and had new CDs in his truck. He must really love this creature, she thought. She must look just right. She must have a smile with no warning label.

She imagines this woman somewhere in the city, AC working just right in her car, crouching real low, mouse-lips ready.

She watches the clock. Not to complicate, she knits, bakes cornbread, dances away the ice inside her fingers.

Sam is texting mouse-woman. Telling her something in finger language. She thinks of them shagpiling, layering each other up with marshmallow filling.

The dog is the only one of them not on the verge of disappearing. Her face resembles a house. Sometimes Sam walks around the dog with his waterproof smile.

"We got ourselves a fine-looking show-dog, with zero work ethic," he says.

The rescue animals were a mistake, one might conjecture, but when in love with animals, there is simply no turning back.

TEA PARTY

UNDERGROUND, a tea party has commenced—a city-full of Dumbo-eared family members.

"Your name was Tim," she reminded him. "Timothy... You and me were married." She realized he had stopped listening and imagined him plunging down a hole or into a box.

"Okay, hold on..." She closed the box gently. Wrapped him in tissue paper recycled from Christmases past.

"When your husband becomes a rodent," she typed into Google, hoping for simple instructions.

Long ago, he explained, his family carried disease. He was simply scurrying down the pipes, trying to get back home.

CALIFORNIA TOWNS

THE highway stops, and her brain gets off. It doesn't know what town it's in. It sees luxury delis, happy families with gold dogs. A rich, California town reminds a woman of her age.

She remembers kissing the one in Idaho, the sunlight on his shoulders when she dug her nose in to his skin, how she sucked in that warmth. Ever since she was little, her feet were cold.

"Have you always been a furnace?" she asked. He would never reply, but in the middle of the night he took her under his big, meaty wing.

* * *

She knows she was deeply disturbed. She should wear a flashing red light. She does not ever want to be on this highway again.

But she says, "Jesus Christ, this feels good to me." Love is a dumbass in an old, red car, sputtering even going the right speed.

"Get cranking," she tells her body, too old for any of it. But she's got her foot on the gas.

MOOD RING

WHEN the sun came out I took off five layers. I felt naked and free, ready to show him the foot. It had changed again, like a mood ring, a naked foot right there in the middle of the living room. He'd just returned from his jog, twenty miles, and there was my foot. The room got still. My husband, the violinist, skinny and quick, a ferret. The room hot and sad, the sofa we'd picked because it was so cozy we just fit.

I kissed the top of his head. "Ouch!" he said. He used to have stacks of hair. I'm sorry about how things turned out, I said, but he knew this already. He was sorry too. Of course. He scooted away and looked out the window. His bald head was a magnet for beauty. There was a new woman on the block, with a Stradivarius body, the kind he had always wanted to play.

HI, HI, HI

AT first they felt zippy and free, his bird-night summer e-mails. One e-mail would say just a few warm words, trail off, be gone it seemed— but then, surprise! An hour later, ten more, like bugs over water. And it was never one *hi*. It was *Hi, hi, hi!* For months, she'd ignore the stabbing feeling of her recent divorce, would call the cat over to her desk. She liked the solidity of the large cat's moon-like presence while she read his words carefully, one at a time.

His e-mails were funny, but also a bit sad. There was often an anecdote about his old, limping dog, or his wife's unfriendly new cat.

Eventually, she asked him to describe what came next.

Well, hey, I'll be alone at the river cottage next weekend by myself (maybe) so then I might actually talk on the phone! he wrote. Along with this e-mail was a photo of himself in an under-shirt, sitting on a bed.

So, yeah, I'm muddling through these days, reading, and, well, yeah, drinking, he said. *But life, life goes on... sigh... How are you?* he wrote, and asked her for a topless photo before they spoke on the phone, if they actually did. It might be good for her self-esteem, he suggested. "I'm not wonderful on the phone, just warning you," he said.

Anyway, they would have to settle for photos. One time he said it straight out. Because it was all there was, at least for now. "But photos can really perk things up," he said.

She didn't agree, and felt that sending him some dumb-looking naked photos of herself wouldn't help. Because once, he had sent her unasked-for photos of himself wearing only a lopsided camping hat, the lower part of his body shadowy and strange.

And once he sent her something she wanted too much and she thought for days and then weeks and probably a whole year about why it moved her, a very short video of him singing off-key with his guitar, and how close she felt to his air, how close they would feel in one warm place on one scented night under purple stars, a deep-ruby moon, because they could do that with her color adjuster, and she would pull off her shoes he would see how small and right her feet were for his true life but only when it was dark, and she would slurp him up inside the warm lake. He would sigh, the water would be moving and something might bite or sting, and even then, they would kiss for hours, would push their millions of written words together.

And they never really stopped. Even years later, his occasional e-mails zipped into her life, sadder and funnier and stranger. A photo of him looking a bit deflated, like someone's grandfather waving from a bed—chirping, *Hi, hi, hi.*

PEACE OFFERING

WHEN I can't fall asleep I walk past the harbour where the ferries slumber fitfully. At the newsstand, I flip through the Spiderman magazines. The manager wears dark circles and Ferris wheel earrings, smiles like a crack in the wall. When my husband disappeared, I told myself he'd always thought of himself as a superhero. I imagined him sliding between the invisible openings of a nicer woman's walls, late at night. Fasting in the morning, waltzing over to Clement Street for dim sum late in the afternoon.

At my last checkup, in the waiting room, I browsed National Geographic. Male water spiders. I'd been waiting for my husband to leave me, I just hadn't known it.

The doctor was optimistic, told me I could come back in six months instead of monthly. Called it "watchful waiting." Not technically remission yet. The hole where my breast used to be was a cozy cave when he touched it.

Back home, my museum of domesticity, I gaze at framed reminders. Snapped moments in which I look sort of happy, but waiting for something else. The double rainbow we spotted in the desert after the huge argument on our honeymoon. The smiling photo of my husband at Pike's Market, his fingers curled over a leg of Dungeness crab, waving its body at me like a peace offering. I wondered if the doctor knew about those spiders, how the males only mate with females larger than themselves. They eat the smaller females they have no interest in.

MY KINGDOM FOR A DOG

SHE whisked the air and pointed her toes like a ballet dancer. Stretch the tendons, movement and method. Because she wanted to wear high heels again someday. Or even to walk limpless. Or to walk.

Since the Segway had run over her foot, she had been lying around, three months of TV in bed. It hadn't done much for her figure or her self-esteem. "But you want the foot (post-surgery) to be able to fold and unfold," he said.

Motion isn't something you know the importance of, until you find yourself lying like a sloth in bed, no longer incorporating air, unable to say hello to the world or go out for scrambled eggs, or own a dog, or even to see dogs, to watch them play. Wasn't everything better with dogs?

"My kingdom for a dog," he said. He used to say this to himself, and then he would change it sometimes and say, "My kingdom for a brown piece of toast."

When the female foot is broken in three places, there are not many ways to drizzle life back into it, but it can be done by combining methods. "You will never," the doctor said, "walk barefoot on sand." Big whoop.

The dust of life settles, but not much else happens.

ANIMAL PROBLEMS

"THE problem with you," he said, "is that your cat is fat. Very fat."

"Fine. Make fun of me and my cat," I said.

I'd been kissing him so much that the tip of my nose was bruised. Later, the tip bled. It bled all night and soiled our top sheet and woke me up so that we made love all night again.

In the morning, there was coffee. In the mirror I was a woman with a black-tipped nose. No coffee could cure it. Makeup could not hide such a scab and bruise. I hung my nose down, looked at the floor.

"How have you hurt your nose?" he asked.

"On you," I said.

"Well, that is what a person who has a fat cat would do," he said.

UNDER BLACKLIGHT

You would hate it if you knew how many times I apply lipstick now that you're gone. I'm putting it on, like, every five minutes to get through the next fifteen, though I know they use fish scales to make it, and it's like killing fish to put on lipstick for no reason. Nobody usually sees my champagne-grape stained lips except myself, and two adorable medical professionals.

If I had been a cat you probably would have kept me forever, even with an incurable disease. I think about that every time I clean the litter pan, especially late at night. I clean it too often because it makes the cats love each other more, and also because I can smell how sad I really am in the unpleasant odor of their piss, which I've read glows under black light.

In bed, my eyelids behave like cheap polyester drapes, unable to keep out the light. I wake from dreams about us walking nowhere... covered with butterflies. I can taste you with my feet the way butterflies taste leaves and flowers. Without you here, I notice too much about how the town is changing, new money moving in, teenage girls with their rubbery, flat stomachs. They walk around cold-eyed, like billboards about nothing.

Sometimes, I drive to the Taste It where they use organic bags. As I shop, I try not to gawk at girl's stomachs like I used to try not to stare at perfect front lawns. If I had a flat stomach, and a perfect lawn, and if I were not dying—you might have stayed here on my sofa, drinking beer and burping to mark your territory.

I'm a sloth, it's what we had in common. And the fact that our left eyes feel much more connected to the intuitive parts of our brains than our right eyes do!

Also, the first time we made love, I remember how we talked about the fact that bulls are really color blind, and how a red garment has nothing to do with their rightful anger. How just having to cope with a cape being waved at you by some short murderer dressed up like a kid on Halloween would be bad enough.

The young doctor took my pulse this morning, prescribed yoga. He had stubble on his shin, and Teva sandals—like you. This guy, this doctor, made me blush when he said he liked my cockroach tattoo. He walked out to get the nurse, held her hand and brought her in to see it. She had a cute hair cut, neon blue eye shadow. She laughed, said random. I told them why cockroaches fascinate me, that they can live for weeks with their heads cut off.

They looked at each other, seemed to connect without touching—as if this were all about them.

WAGER

SHE asks him to say what she is wagering when she dresses this way. She is wearing a filmy orange negligee. He says that she looks "like a pincher" in orange. He doesn't even know what he is trying to say, what he means, but it feels right: "pincher."

"Princess?" she asks. "I look like a princess to you?"

"No, I said 'pincher'. That it pinches to see you this way."

"Really? As if I am like... I dunno, a human crab?" she asks.

"Okay, you're a princess, you are a gorgeous fucking princess," he says.

"I am not," she says.

When she stays over, the night creeps up like a tentative dog.

"Do you want to make love?" he asks her in the morning, while the sun is still soft.

KRAZY GLUE

SHE betrays her husband with the new dog. Adoring the dog, kissing his glossy ears. In the kitchen a flood of pain, two aspirin and her ears twitching from the explosive sounds of a party up the block. Tired couples hip-bumping, laughing, that someday they'll be too tired to do this... She imagines the street opening, a man gazing into her window, stroking a red cigarette. Her husband is up on the roof trying to patch things with glue. He reads up there, insists it's safe, even at night with a flash-light. The kids off at college and she's in her bathrobe and slippers letting the dog out to pee on the lawn, making quiet noises for him, "coo coo coo... " She pulls at her hair, thin as corn thread, and wants to tell her doctor about the grass she can't walk on anymore because it is uneven, the black way she feels about that, and how she imagines herself in a movie. She betrays her husband by holding the cat to her lips.

SETTLING

HE took my hand, led me to the bathroom, opened the door and slipped in. The bathroom was dark. Through the partially opened window, an apartment with a yellow breakfast nook. His breath was on my mouth with the smell of fruit and white wine, sweet and sour sauce. This was where he felt safest; bathrooms, closets, tiny, ridiculous places.

Earlier that night, at a movie, I'd listened to him eating un-buttered popcorn. How each piece squeaked in his teeth. I believed I'd grow to hate this sound, and the idea made me want to plant my hand on his knee, which I did.

There were many ways to love, and to be loved, and none of them were just the way you dreamed as a child. My mother had been relieved to lounge around in an old, stained bathrobe, watch the news and fall asleep after my father left. Some people don't want the worries of entanglement, Mom had said. Some people prefer the music of their own lives.

ROLLING OUT

I woke up, rolled out of bed, and felt beautiful. I called the man I'd met online and told him that I really lived a lot closer than he thought. "I'm wearing elevator shoes," he said. "Because I'm tall in my soul." Fine with me. When I looked in the mirror, I just had to blink. I'd woken up with goldfish lips, long blond hair down to my knees, and island blue peep-holes. I looked like a fuck-me doll. I stood there staring until I began to laugh.

What kind of joke is this? I said to myself in the mirror. Who asked for this, anyway?

I walked to the kitchen and started to sing. Birds flew in through the window and landed on my shoulders. I did a little dance kick and felt myself rising. I rose like Jesus right inside my living room. I hadn't even gotten to the kitchen yet. What do saints like me eat? I asked myself. What does it take to fuel such a gorgeous machine? I thought about this for a while, then called your old number. It didn't ring. I talked to you about this new self of mine. "Hi, I think you might want to love me again now," I said.

AS IN MANY OF HER CORNY STORIES

SHE wanted to sit behind him on a saddle, to let the horse of time ride them off into the sunset.

In the light of the moon they walked from one bookstore to the next. He said something kind about her childish socks. She looked down at them, they reflected the moon back up into her eyes, which normally ached from reading. She asked him to hold her hand and he did. She said his fingers felt like an envelope. He said, at least they're not rectangularly shaped.

They both laughed, because they were old. They had lied to each other about their ages. Imagine even trying to get into a saddle, she said to herself. She asked him if he remembered playing the King.

"You were certainly my Queen," he said. She accepted that she probably felt royal to him one night, or more, during that time.

She felt a sudden urge to see the Big Dipper, holding his hand, for them both to see it and say what it was they were feeling. But there they were, in San Francisco, near City Lights Bookstore, and looking into the sky there were only vague pinpricks of light.

The country, where they could see stars properly! This was where she needed to stand with him!

But first, she wanted to feel his shirt against her face. She asked him, and he let her. While she nuzzled against him, he pet her hair with his papery hands and lifted her droopy face to his, studying her eyes.

He said they looked pretty much like he had imagined five years earlier. She suggested they squat down to pretend they could still be children.

BLUE TONGUED SKINK

HE wanted me to have a purpose in this world. Having a baby would get me out of bed and cooking, he said. Bending over, planning dinners. He probably also wanted me to be more awake, not just lying in bed, as I did most days.

Too late. I had put my money down on an exotic lizard. A baby did not sound nearly as interesting. The pet store had my deposit, and I was lying in bed planning my future with the blue-tongued skink. He lived at the store. They tended to be slow to adopt out. I just needed the glass cage and the U.V. lights, a large bag of sand and an endless supply of insects. I had photos of skinks everywhere now, the inside and the outside of my phone. I was considering a reptile tattoo, and all I could think about was how such cool, smooth skin would feel around my shoulder, like an arm, or a hand. How much warmer than anything else I might happen to love.

CURSE

THE old superstition says that when a clock strikes during wedding vows it's bad luck. She hadn't noticed a clock at the in-and-out chapel so this must have something to do with the cake knife her husband pointed at his chest on their honeymoon. How he looked at the ground as if he'd made a horrible mistake.

She saw the tall, indignant figure of a grandfather clock in her dream, its sickening, satisfied face. Her real grandfather used to trap her on his lap. She needed to jump up, to jump away from him, to spring from his drunk, sunken love—but he held her there.

"I'm stockpiling your kisses," he'd whisper with old-man breath. "I'm fortifying my castle."

DANCER

SHE lived far away, down near the ballpark. I rolled out of bed and right into my car because I couldn't stand how my weekends involved no mercy. How when I woke up I needed to figure things out.

Once I got to her place we drank coffee and she showed me her favorite baskets. She danced for me again, and time flowed. I was reserved, but she was a ham. Something to do with how joy lived in Al Pacino movies. We both had a thing about Pacino.

I tried to remember how he looked when he wasn't doing something violent. My own love scenes were so long in the past, I'd become an eel, slithering around the edges, poking into places I didn't belong.

I thought of it as the submarine, my friends' SOMA Loft, and how there was something like joy in the affected way she danced, a beautiful kind of self-consciousness.

Yo, I said, I'm here for the show! She twisted and swayed as if I were someone important. Later, she leaned her head on my shoulder and I rested my head on hers, and we settled there like that, my arms stiff and annoyed and unable to do anything tender. I thought of us as a two-headed creature, her curls much nicer and neater than mine, tied back by a bright red babushka, her face with fewer lines than mine.

When the clock crept around to noon, I felt the strain of my husband not calling, but knowing where I was. I had no desire to go, to leave her lying on her chaise lounge with a grin and a promise of next Sunday, again. She said it was fine, she was tired, she needed to workout anyway, dancing or Judo or yoga or pilates. To bring up a sweat, she said. Sweat.

SCARS OF TEMPEH

OUR towels were frayed and the dog was sleeping in the middle of this scuttled floor. I did my job: pizza ordered, no salad. The youngest cat yowling his baby sound, hairball imminent.

The overlapping waves were why we moved here, the sky and the Cliff House. And the feeling that this was fresh. Memories rise from the mind like lint.

The day I drove by the Cliff House, so happy on the dumb curves.

We didn't own one dish, but we had a wok and could fry scars of tempeh, enough to say we were alive. Just enough to want an orange sunset together, leaning.

RESTLESSNESS

I saw you dance to a Madonna song at the Discovery. You looked like a young Clark Kent. Those glasses next to your nose taunted me into drinking more than I was good with.

It didn't stay in, but what the hell. I glowed and we kissed under the awning, and you said I smelled like your favorite pillowcase, after your molar was pulled and the pillowcase was soaked in blood.

I think it was then you smoothed my thighs, and I let you feel the bumps under my sweater. And then you went back and danced to another, and you have tenderizer hands. Can I order some?

You are never where I am at any other time. There is nothing I can take a chance on.

I will wear nylon over my flaws for you, shaving my legs more often. Just the thought of your sly mouth on mine. My legs so smooth they feel infantile.

Your name started with a consonant, but I can't remember it now. My man is in the world's deepest sleep, and you have the shoe that fits. Why can't we pretend we are bunny rabbits? It's doubtful you'll see this, but I've got the warren ready.

INFIDELITY

HE watched her again that day, her face, her features, something that might change. The way she watched him back, eyes like blue dragonflies hovering near a rock. He brushed the hair from his eyes, tilted his face to the right like a chain-smoking waitress. What'll you have? he wanted to say. Chips with cheddar? Sex with a kiss? Words he could use with other women, but not with her.

He had nobody to talk to, and the words gathered in his throat like angry tourists, pushing each other out.

"Near the trail, I saw a yellow bird," he said. That sounded ignorant. Birds weren't yellow— they had a yellow breast or a yellow wing tip. There was no way to know if she heard, so he watched her mouth. Sometimes it looked cruel, other times it made him want to laugh. He stared at her nose, a long, crazy nose—so large that it should have pulled her gaze down, but it balanced just right.

He closed his mouth because it felt dangerous to speak. Better to accept fate, to listen to the sound of his criminal heart. Because he almost said it. He almost said it to her expressionless gaze, that she would never love him back.

THE DOG SEATED NEXT TO ME

My heart has city scum all over it, a coat of frosting. I wear it outside of me like a necklace, because it's dangerous. Sometimes I imagine it glowing in the dark. It used to make me troubling but lovable.

Way out here in the country, they have dogs, firepits and stars.

"We keep the windows open all night long to hear the bug music," the man who used to want me but is now my friend laughs. As he roasts the hotdogs, his gaze buzzes around the garden.

He passes me the communal salad bowl filled with kale, sunflower seeds and strawberries.

"Fresh, really sweet," he says. "You can't get these berries in the city."

I remember when that mattered, what he said and how he said it to me. The way his lips moved in time with each other.

Later, he asks if he can hold the heavy fruit bowl for me while I serve myself.

"I'm not that frail," I say.

He's seeing a much younger woman now, so I talk to the dog seated next to me.

STRAY OTTERS

THE air smells like charity in this town.

Down by the river, it smells like dog.

My husband gave up on my toothpick smile, left, found true happiness. He had the kind of pain that begs morphine. I got bigger and rounder, named myself Daffodil. Threw away most of my belongings. Felt right.

These days I look for rare animals everywhere. Every once in a while stray otters show up in the river. They tend to clump. Perhaps I'll hear a few in-concert.

Me and a few friends, we enjoy karaoke night, but we know it's useless. We're hobbyists. We've all been struck by worries, and we eat too much cheese. They say cheese is like heroin, that addictive.

Madness, handled correctly, becomes my gift.

WHAT THE DOG THINKS

TODAY she seemed to be chasing her tail. I mean, chasing herself into a bad mood. At 11AM she was wearing her astral nightgown and her Jupiter slippers. She needed a project. I heard her say this to a few people on the phone. Did I mention that her hair was really orange this time? It was only pretty at night.

When she talks on the phone, and I listen... It's not eavesdropping because she speaks so loudly. It can be heard all over the planet, a lot of what she says. And she was petting my head a bit during some of that conversation. She said, I'm tired of being a wife. It's not a job I'm good at.

She cried a bit, and the poor friend on the other end of the line must have been upset. She said she was nothing but a broken link, that she loved getting drunk in bars and being courted, that she had an uncontrollable fear of old people. That she was a horrible person, a horrible wife, a terrible daughter, ready to make a landing on a new betrayal every week.

That is what she said.

It sounded true to me, but nobody knows what is true here. After she hung up, she hurried off to meet a man at the coffee shop. How do I know? I saw her put on green eye-shadow, the color she swore hurried love along. She's nothing but rude when she primps, scooting me away. She's forgotten to love me so regularly now that I've started taking it from the fat white cat. This cat! She even loves my awful breath, says that my bigness obscures the actual sensation. She follows me around these days, and I admit to liking it. But man, is she white—and fat!

DIFFERENT KIND OF WOMAN

AFTER your secret visit to the SPCA, there is a nasty smell on your jeans. Like death. Your husband is simply not enthusiastic about adopting more rescue animals. But that's it. He's never home after work. He and his coworkers are out at the pub complaining about the 1% with their private jets. They drink without you until you have to call a cab to get him home.

After Christmas, he talks about beer-making, and this helps keep him in. He wonders about what it would be like to have a partner who plays golf. He tells you this, as if it's funny. *This would be a very different kind of woman*, he says.

You still want to rescue an animal, but you don't say it anymore. In fact, he smiles at the thought of you looking like everybody else. You—a grabby, American woman. Sports, weapons and infants. He's overcome with giggles.

STAINS

SHE was wondering about what to do with her stained dishtowels. They kept popping out of the drawers. She'd reach for an awkward potholder, and out would spring a ruined dishtowel. She could not seem to throw them out or use them to polish her silverware or boots. They reminded her of her ex-husband. For a little while, when she was young, he had made her happy. Almost ten years ago. She'd gotten over it, but kept the dishtowels.

She was figuring out how to keep this date out of her apartment. Some things were too personal. What did she know of him? He was allergic to sun. "I'm allergic," his profile said, "to warmth, and to anything soft." He had just moved back to San Francisco after trying life out in Milwaukee where fat people lived. He was back from the dead—that's how he put it.

"I like the skinny, silent women," he said. Nancy understood. She liked a skinny, unfriendly kind of man. The kind who stood there saying nothing. A man who didn't wear pork-pie hats. A man who could drink

all night, drive to Costco, and not throw up.
A man who dreamed of making love with a
mermaid.

FLUSTERED

WHY wouldn't he want to make love to her? For God's sake! She could yodel. Perform bird calls on cue, the way real birds understood them. Could fold a stained dishtowel into a hat. Was gypsy-pretty, had a little dog-friendly hatchback car. Was great at making people laugh at her ex-husband's phobias. Would say: "I loved him so much that I had to divorce him." So many gifts.

The man who wouldn't love her wrote documentary films. Swam in the San Francisco Bay. Didn't worry about poverty. Worked for National Geographic. Was good at living sparely. Loved The Eels. Danced and flirted with her. Shared whiskey from his flask. "I love your velvet hat," he said. "I'd like to take you out sometime." Very old fashioned. Sweet. They walked around the city all day and night.

Did it have to do with her childhood? With her mother who needed to be a father. With her sisters who said she was useless. With dysfunctional dogs. Runaway cats. The blushing disease. No drinking habit to speak of. A senti-

mental belief in God, an embarrassing love for
Disneyland. Separation anxiety. The chronic,
lifelong worry of how it will feel to be old and
alone.

IN THE MIDDLE OF NOWHERE

SOMETIMES, she wanted to run away from her husband, but she could not live without their Labradoodle, Timmy.

At the dog park she sat Indian-style picking her split ends and remembering the maze of approval inside her lover's laugh and then later, under the covers, how he said, "You are my thing."

Timmy had watched them at first, which made her shy, but then he'd fallen asleep, paw around Squeaky Duck. There was no guilt. She had not given it a second thought because Timmy's snoring made them laugh, all part of the fun that was happening. Even the next morning, Timmy was rolling over and squirming to play, the way she had been. It meant all creatures were the same. Dogs did not hate what they saw or didn't see, and they loved whatever they smelled, especially if it was unusual. But all she really wanted, now, was to run away.

Her husband knew—they all knew—that she'd never leave that dog. And her husband, well, he was addicted to Wii golf now, but that didn't matter. What did matter was the sound of him playing that game in the living room, and how comfortable it made her feel about nothing.

LIES

Iᴛ's something to do with rules unwillingly broken, trophies not won, disobedient body parts. The signs you ignored when he lay on top of you like a stiff blanket.

The sound-soother is off. I don't any longer require tenderness and my big audition was years ago. Let's not use the word "delicious" when we remember his buttered lips, the way he said my jeans smelled like a forest, how our honeymoon ended with vanilla nut coffee, pleasant and dumb. When we swam out into the sea of yard sales, flea markets, superstores. Whatever fit inside our little red car.

THE WEEK I BECAME OLD

I met him for lunch at The Hive. He had black curly hair and a strained smile. I tried to relax, smoothed my skirt, patted my blouse down, moved my feet toward his.

I had become old just that week, no longer wanted to even try to be open, felt useless and befuddled. Yet I had found a space on the street away from the parking meters, two hours to get myself enlivened. It was a relief to see that he was as anxious as me, with a scrunched look on his rootlike face. Was I taboo?

Did you take the bus to get here? he asked.

No, I don't take the bus, I said. Did you? I didn't even know how to take a bus.

No, I just came from work. I only have an hour. And then back to work. Sorry.

No, that's okay, I said. He started telling me his story. He was in the middle of a divorce, his wife had thrown him out—"like an overcooked noodle," he said, the way she threw out his old CDs, mementos, family photographs. "She

MEG POKRASS

finally (quote) uncluttered her life," he said. "I was one of the things she no longer wanted."

The energy flow between us was taking its time, trying not to aggravate our conditions, but it was happening. At that moment, I saw him in an old photograph. He reminded me of the sherbety days of high school, the salty skin of the first boy I had kissed behind the library. And the second boy, and the third boy, and the fourth boy I had kissed behind the library as though I were becoming a technician, a kissing scientist. Until somebody alerted my mother about my "problem." After which the kisses stayed with me, slid into my pockets like gum wrappers.

And yet this man was ruined. Thrown out, discarded. His wife had been holding him, and she was ready to move on.

SHOW BUSINESS

YESTERDAY I almost tripped over a man lying in the road. "What is wrong with you?" I asked. "Show business," he said. He was not exaggerating—his eyes were really just holes with marbles in them.

He told me about his ex-girlfriend, a woman he'd met on the stage, an actress and dancer. "Her eyes were homes of silent prayer to me," he said. Water dripped down from his holes.

I felt I could tell him anything, and so I did. My boyfriend had an awful way of making a living, I said. He juggled stunned live birds and then got rid of them. "Juggling living birds for crowds," I said.

He shook little white petals from his shirt and stood up. "I won't be had," he said.

"Neither will I," I said. And then we held hands, and made promises we'd someday break.

MEG POKRASS

WAITING FOR THE WALRUS MAN

I was shivering out on the curb waiting for the fella who resembled a friendly walrus to drive up and take me for whiskey. This would be my second date with a man who resembled a sea mammal, but at least I wasn't going to be slogging the Christmas alone. Not many on the website were free and ready to rumble.

Earlier in the day, my dog Riley had slipped in with a dead pheasant in his mouth and I nearly stepped on it getting out of bed. *Why?* I said. He dropped the corpse at the base of our Christmas tree. *Why not?*

This was the dog who'd infected my marriage. The scapegoat for our divorce, but I couldn't hold it against him. He was the only living creature who needed me. I had been born, it seemed, to care for this murderous canine.

In the litter of Christmas cards, a glossy one from my ex. He had remarried. He and his new honey had a successful frozen yogurt franchise. "Come by for a free double scoop," his card said. The leering snowman on their Xmas card looked like it was made of milk balls. My ex had evolved into a happier human with less nuclear debt, no rescue animals. His wife probably had no sinus infections.

So why shouldn't a fella with a walrus face make me tingle? I sighed, waiting and waiting, sitting on the curb. I sang a few carols. Time drifted past. Maybe the fella had lost my address. Perhaps I dreamt the whole thing up.

THE BITE

You didn't know he had escaped. You thought he was a terrific dog, smitten with you, looking at you like you were someone he could enjoy the sun with. He licked your face, and you liked it too much. Nobody had licked your face in years.

He followed you down a shaded path. If he could talk, he may have said something about the "view" (meaning your ass).

He leaned against the large, graffitied tree, pulled you in to him with his wolf-blue eyes. You pet him, you sang to him as he cocked his head.

His bite was deep. It felt wonderful. Blood, your own blood, leaked onto the gray-green grass, under the redwood tree. Right near the old yellow house. A place rented for weddings. A place that had been one of your favorite sights.

The dog never came back. Instead, his owner called you on the phone and screamed at you, growled a death cry that would stop chopped ice. Told you that you were ruining her life.

You shivered and tucked yourself in near the other animals, the ones you knew better.

A week later, a postal truck delivered some boxes. The owner sent you perfectly wrapped parts of her dismembered dog, parts that she wanted buried far away. The last box you opened was the one holding its tag. For a few more years, you would wear it against your skin.

EASTER IN TEXAS

It was Easter in Texas, and I was in bed with a college professor, an amateur golfer. He hummed in his sleep. I was dreaming about my husband, at home in California with our sick dog and the SUV.

In this dream my husband was a pirate, stealing from my sisters, burying the loot in his parents' yard.

My lover told me that in his dream he was teeing off at Pebble Beach just as I yelled "Fuck off!" to my husband in mine.

"You with the button to my heart, you with the California life, ruined my chance at golf-greatness." Hugging me like an anchor. Later, his ex-wife called to describe the ringing in her ears.

The ecstatic squeals of the home-schooled kids next door with their Easter baskets. How he pushed my hand away, led me to the bedroom as if I had the key. How, at the airport, he said he hoped my husband would let me back in.

"Don't give up on me," he said, my lipstick all over his face.

Back at home in California, weekends as lonely as Christmas, my husband and his long stringy words, sounds that made me sick.

In dreams, I tell my doctor, me and the professor are still in bed. It's always Easter in Texas, I explain. We sit close to each other, watching the walking wounded who love us too much.

PRESCRIPTION

THE last appointment, my doctor popped the question—asked me to pet-sit and house-sit for him while he traveled to Florence—described his wooded wonderland cottage on Mount Tamalpais and his arthritic dog, Jeeves.

I'm dying very quickly, and the sweet chemicals in candy and diet sodas are comforting, so the first thing I think about is if there would be a convenience store nearby, so deep in the woods. Nobody believes that I'm dying from such a sad, and rare disorder—one that doesn't have a name. Only the doctor knows what is really wrong with me, but he says there is no name for this fatal illness.

Sometimes, he'll begin "you see..." then, change the trail of the conversation to something as impersonal as the local deer population crisis.

"Well, yes of course they are a menace to gardens," I say, "but they don't look evil, that's what is so damn sad I bet?" He doesn't answer which makes me worry that he would shoot them, and I tell myself he wouldn't, being a natural healer.

He said this is a lonely pilgrimage—off to Florence to say goodbye to his former fiancé, a well known visual artist named Sandra who has a rare and fatal blood disease. Her illness has a name, but the name is very long and Latin, and he can't pronounce it. He said it would be easier to sing it, says, "Bella, bella" when he speaks of her.

"I can take care of the doggie and cottage," I had said, wanting him to perk. He stroked his beard sweetly, as if it were a bunny. I wanted to touch all of the doctor's things. I wanted to lie in his sheets.

I've done many things the doctor will not approve of since moving in, like turning on the heat in the frigid mornings, and removing his aggressive wind chimes. I am bored with his beautiful house, the whimsical trickle of a natural creek in the yard that honest-to-God polliwogs swim in. I'm on Pluto, or maybe I have landed in Carmel before it was ruined and turned into a theme park. I hate authentic character I've decided, the master bedroom smelling like vintage sweat and pine, salty stuff I'll never smell fresh from his skin unless I grab him while he's jogging, in which case I would risk being abandoned as his patient.

I feel annoyed by his creviced leather sofa, forest green corduroy chairs, Pennsylvania Dutch braid rugs. The only bright spot is Jeeves, the doctor's ten year old golden retriever who follows me everywhere wishing I were the doctor. We have talks about why the doctor dresses so well, when all the other doctors look schlumpy. "Do you think he's vain?" I ask Jeeves, who looks unsure about everything.

I'm not getting enough fruit he'd say, am getting sick from energy bars and diet cokes. I am often thinking about what it would be like to be naked under the llama rug when the doctor gets home all stricken with grief.

Since living in the doctor's cottage, I've been imagining the shape of his fingers while chopping vegetables. Picking just one finger would be hard, like selecting a puppy from a box. Some people fall into the trap of the rice farmer obsessed with growing apples. And it's true, I've grown and cultivated men all my life—but this one will not thrive in my soil. It's time to move on.

I water each of the doctor's daisy bushes carefully, do not flood their roots. I talk to his plants so they don't die while he's gone. Jeeves waddles out and plunks next to me to sit in the sun.

WHAT THE DEAD WANT

THERE are so many dead people in her life, especially in this house. They float around and exaggerate. They want to see something sexy. That nightgown? they say. They miss eating berries. They're sure she'll be okay. They say wonderful things about what you might do here on earth. They should have taken more lovers, had more beach weekends, seen more foreign films. They ask for autographs from the living.

BUS VIBRATIONS

THE vibrations of the California bus wake me from another dream, the kind of dream that makes me hop on my better foot until it sweats. The bus is gassy and sounds as though it's saying 'oops'.

People get off the bus looking sorry and mad and clumsy, interrupting each others bodies, robbing each other of something.

I can't shoot my words straight anymore... and it's as though someone has turned the electricity off.

Everyone knows, how a man's eyes dart like bullets toward soft new hills. Young men wear rain-repellent clothing and do not use umbrellas anymore. In movies they own iguanas and parrots and have affairs with funny women played by funny women.

But today, what matters is that I finally own a cell phone, and that my cell phone, when it rings, sounds like a cat fight, or like an affair, and sure—someone will like that. So I get off the bus and I am in the wrong place again.

INTEGRITY

NANCE lost her integrity years ago when she slept with everyone, but promised them nothing. It would have been more sensible to promise something, but never sleep with them.

By the time she was diagnosed, she had lost her husband. To him, it made no sense. The weirdness of it all. Nonsense, like a husband and wife who get a divorce even though they love each other.

* * *

And then, after years on her own, Nance met Bob. Bob had been recruited to help plant a tree in a neighbor's yard.

Nance's ex had not been handy, couldn't even put up a shelf without breaking it. Did that mean she shouldn't miss him?

She waved at the tree-planting man on the way to her car, determined to stop confusing men with sex. She woke up all sparkly-eyed and ready to hit the ground, determined not to confuse anyone. It was about as exciting as getting up before dawn to tackle the tax forms.

* * *

Bob was, no doubt, married. In the old days that meant Nance would plot to seduce him. She'd confuse a man on his wedding day. Or in the middle of an anniversary. Her smile would make a man lose his bearings or feel he already knew her, sure he'd slept with her already so it didn't count.

Her smile was the thing. It reminded people of their grandmothers or their favorite nieces. Familiar but provocative. She'd loved being alive. She had felt that this was what she'd been put on earth to do... to confuse other humans.

* * *

Bob had such a warm look that Nance was ready to say hello—nicely, sisterly—while checking his ring finger. You might have said that she was ready to *begin again*.

She practiced, taking her cat into her arms, snuggling him until she felt tenderness begin, like a run in her stocking. Like an ant making its dangerous way toward home.

WHAT ARE YOU DOING, FRIEND?

His voice tender and sore. Not angry, like the photo. Not turning on this moment.

The woman lives in there still. What are you doing? she whispers, because he is not the him that can be spoken to.

This is surely a ghost. She walks around the house barefoot, looking at stacks of problems. Touching his absence.

What are you doing, friend? she might ask his light blue eyes that look like birds.

VINTAGE

MOST women hated her on sight because (her therapist explained) she was small-boned and dainty. He said this was an animal-thing, nobody's fault. Women, especially tall ones, would just never like her. Men however, felt protective toward her. She found it both wonderful and worrisome, the way her therapist hugged her a lot.

Round hipped and full breasted, she wore 1950's beaded sweaters and swing coats. Modern clothing didn't fit right, so she shopped at the rare, vintage places.

Every day, large women would smirk at her, as though she were lint on a hat. Trying to escape the tall ones, walking like a tunnel of wind, she'd find herself on 68th and Broadway instead of 86th and Broadway where she lived.

Protective men followed her carefully, offered her bus fare, suggested where she could find a bar. "Maybe you could use a drink," they'd say. She appeared so lost. How could they help? That is what they always wanted to know.

Until the time, years later, when a nicely

dressed man with a long, thin dog on a pretty red leash asked her if she needed assistance. She'd been standing directionless at a stop sign near the third Korean market on Broadway, clutching a bag of cilantro. The wind was picking up. Her basket purse was blooming with scarves and hats.

The man had said "Excuse me. Are you lost?" and she remembered answering, "Yes, very." His eyes flitted briefly to her basket and his nose twitched. In the old days, he would have noticed her sweater.

He patted his dog and said, "Well then," and walked away, as if he had no desire to protect her.

Those hips could warm her bones, she thought. She stood there, mesmerized by the feeling of smallness. As he walked away, she noticed the lush, middle-aged pads around his hips and the way he seemed to be aiming toward something solid.

SOMETHING SHE
NEEDED TO KNOW

THE boy in third grade who left a Mickey
Mouse ring and a love note in her desk. The
garage door with thousands of spiders' nests,
nobody to wash them down. Her mother
looking different in California, hair tipped
blond, smoking near the telephone. Her father
in Maryland, the wrinkled map of his hands.
Sneaking out of the house at dawn, hoping to
get kidnapped, to be returned to sender. The
boy pulling her into the bathroom, telling her
she could watch. Butter stains on clothing, the
gift for ruining things, even the potted cactus.
The plane to Pennsylvania, landing in snow,
the hearse carrying her father to a perfect hole.
Her cousin so changed with new huge breasts,
glaring at her mother. Her aunt saying Why
did you treat him like that? God's voice in the
dark of the hotel room, talking to her while
her mother snored away. Songs on the radio
like Take Me In Your Arms and Rock Me,
something she needed to know. Her father's
moon face smiling from so many brown frames

on the wall; holding a dog, holding a trophy, being a boy before growing up into her terrible parent. How she would have wanted to play with him then. And the warm way she feels when she thinks of the peeing boy's body. How her father, in the form of different boys, would always make her watch.

CIDER

MORNINGS, the person in the mirror hardly resembled the woman she used to admire.

"My god," she said. "I look like a distant relative!"

"Do you feel good?" Bob asked. "That's what matters."

"Right. Just thinking that maybe I should cut back on the cider a bit," she said.

"There's no point in that," Bob said. "Everyone should have such problems."

Sometimes, before she slept, she wandered outside to visit the moon. Her life with Bob felt both heavy and light when she was holding a glass. From such a distance, she could see their house as a lifetime.

Imagine that, she thought. We live in a box.

She leaned against the apple tree, sipping. She hadn't known how intense it would be, brewing their own.

Weeds grew. Days, she drank herbal tea.

"Wait until you taste the new stuff," Bob said, his face distant, elated—sinking his finger into the new batch, spinning it around.

RICE PAPER AND LUCK

In Chinatown they all look hungry. My once-loving husband is visiting his doll, and I'm coasting down Russian Hill in my rusty old car, singing songs nobody remembers. Do you see me slumped in the back of Al Wing's Chinese restaurant, slurping congee with a man who wants me but hasn't got the equipment?

What are we doing here? I say.

He winks, sighs, fondles my knee.

To him, this date is made of rice paper and luck.

He has dumpling cheeks, calls me Dragon Doll, wiggles his chopsticks at my lips.

"Suck this, little bird," he says.

I want to say, How exactly would this work? I imagine him with his jeans around his ankles, me with an instruction manual, and his overcooked noodle.

So I leave us both on the verge of happiness at Al's, our fortune cookies still intact. I'll call this photo "Christmas in Chinatown," fall asleep alone in my car, wrestle with the memory of my ex and me seeing Chinatown for the first time together. Christmas. How happy we were to know that world existed. Lining up at the tofu truck, holding fingers.

NEW DOG

SHE notices him along the walking path, walking a madcap new dog. One he adopted soon after the old one died. She puffs her cheeks into a smile to show approval. In the city, strangers don't use words with each other. Instead, they imitate porcupines. Quills come out. They bubble, move their mouths into lines.

This new, headstrong dog does not seem as though it will ever become gentle, like the old dog was. She believes that one must dispose of the past. That dogs are similar to ex husbands. Moving on is critical. And yet, this new dog really seems the wrong type. It bucks against the man's leash, bounces as if possessed.

This can happen to anyone. There are these problems with memories of dogs we once loved, dogs we will never walk again.

* * *

And yet before her, and she is not making this up, a very attractive man is pulling up next to her in a vintage Beetle. She imagines the way his notched lips would look at a sushi bar, a good one. One that she never goes to anymore. A pass, maybe he is making a pass at her.

"I take it you don't drive," he says, his window slid down, his moon-face beaming.

"Right, " she says, "But, I can see you do."

One man for every three women in California, the stats read. Some kind of exotic fruit, this man. "Fuckit," she says to herself.

"You are pretty when you smile, I'll bet," he says. "But this is just an educated guess."

"Thanks," she says, offering a tiny mouse grin, walking away briskly.

"Bitch," the man says.

The hard part is being a martyr and enjoying it. Organic food and steamed vegetables most nights, masticating for a long time before swallowing. Bird sips of purified water.

She's learning how to be thankful rather than grateful. This is her life's ambition these days. Her friend are obsessed with it, and they say it does wonders for your life once you can actually figure out the sneaky difference between the two feelings. There are classes at the new Community Center in how to get rid of the wrinkles on your face by smoothing out the lines in your soul.

The way she explains it to her son is this: "Since I divorced your father, I've been under cloud-cover, but I'm always thankful that the air here is warm."

Sometimes she sits around the house feeling sorry for herself until she gets a craving for crab. Nothing wrong with being hungry, in fact, hunger presents an opportunity for fullness. She is thankful, not grateful, for the very existence of crab legs, the hidden, perfect meat inside.

* * *

Over at Clownfish, the new downtown sushi joint, she's sitting alone, staring at the fish tornado, proud of herself for taking control.

She's heard about these revolving sushi bars in which you can just grab whatever you want to devour from moving plastic trays. What she wants is a heap of fantasy sashimi that is both very fresh and easy to chew. But it can be hard to know how to spot them while they go whizzing past.

An elegant-looking woman sits near her eating a seaweed salad with triangular chopsticks. "Did you bring your own sticks in?"

she asks the intimidating woman, politely.

On second glance, this is probably the kind of woman who can break a male heart in five pieces, but is not interested in men. "It's often hard to know what kind of fish is zipping past us," the elegant creature says. "Best way through it is to learn to take risks, to be thankful for whatever lands on our plate."

THE RESCUE

HE told her how his parakeets died, all at once, in the middle of a regular day. A bird holocaust. She could see, behind his words, such gorgeous, frantic colour that she held his hand. There were so many stories he'd never tell her about other departures. He was busy trying to make her laugh, reaching for a joke, and it would work! She'd laugh her fluttery heart out, hand it to him from the tip of her tree.

BURRITO

HER new husband is snoring demurely on his side of the bed, wrapped up in a burrito of sheets. She can't find his skin. She lies there awake, thinking about the ex. No matter how bad their problems were, she always relaxed in his smell and the warmth of his skin: he never tamaled himself away. He'd hold her tight against his shoulder until morning. At some point this became intolerable—that only his nocturnal shoulder made them happy together, that all day they'd fight. She told him it made no sense to confuse matters that way. He agreed and withdrew, moving into the living room—his space—for the next two years, sleeping alone with his shoulder empty while they went through the divorce. She still thinks about this at night while her new husband lies away from her, politely, like a ghost.

THE BIG SLEEP

HE was meticulously rude. Sometimes profoundly nice. When we weren't arguing, we'd snuggle under our effective sweat-box comforter, frayed from so many happy and sad years of sex and sweat and dog hair. Outside, the whole world seemed to be tanning and wrinkling.

The police popped in one night to see if our fights were murderous. We'd been arguing loudly in the kitchen about the texture of a birthday cake I'd baked for the twentieth anniversary of our sweet dog's death. It was hard as a rock, and nothing had ever been different. Arguing was part of the cake-eating experience.

When I heard the doorbell ring, I tippy-toed from the kitchen into the bedroom.

"Hello sir, mind if we enter?" a cop-voice said.

"Do you own any weapons, sir?" he asked my husband. It sounded like there were fifteen people, like horses and villagers or showgirls. Lots of feet. A dog toy squeaked. "Whoops!" one of them said.

"With a chef like my bride? Weaponry with this woman here?" then a scratchy minute of silence, my ear to the door. "Where did she go?"

One of the cops let out a giggle. The talkative one sniffed the air, said, "Um. Interesting scent." He was referring to the sweet smell of marijuana.

It was time for me to enter, so I idled into the living room wearing my "Munch Me" shortie night shirt, and my long-nosed barracuda slippers. Not much else. My legs were still shapely, and tan from bronzing gel.

"Hey! I recognize you! I think I knew your mom!" I said to the younger cop. He was adorable, with dirty blond hair and an ape-like neck.

Clicking over to him with my vixen slippers, I looked him over the way Bacall checked out Bogie in *The Big Sleep*.

"You know how to whistle, don't you?" I said, with my full, husky voice. And then I laughed.

He smiled sheepishly. "We didn't mean to disturb your evening, ma'am, just doing our jobs."

"Ha," my husband said. "Who in their right

minds would kill her? Would you kill her?"

After they left, my husband was in fine spirits. He put on Sinatra's "Fly Me To The Moon."

"You have such wonderful moves," he said. Asked me to dance.

BIKE MECHANIC

THEY were kissing on the beach again. She was old enough to be his mother. He lived for his patched-together bikes. Cycled from town to town, free-flowing. Most people knew nothing about bicycle mechanics. He knew everything. She was impressed. She'd given up on having a life. Can you tell? she asked, her lips resting on his hairless belly.

She told him the story. A lifetime ago she had a bike, a husband, a house, a dog. A chubby dog. They were out of milk that morning, so she rode her bike to the grocery store, came home three months later with a dent in her head. She had been married then, living a normal-ish life, worrying about the dog. She could remember the way her husband was, rolling his eyes at her.

If he'd only been a bike mechanic, like you. You're beautiful, she said.

He told her not to think so hard, looped his arms all the way around her waist. His wrists were thick and dark. The bitterness rolled around, made a hum inside her brain as if it had its own gear. She fell asleep in his sandy arms, felt like she was riding home.

LOST TOURIST

It was her high school boyfriend who started the trouble. She was just sixteen. He suggested that she didn't have a normally shaped vagina, his finger skittering around it like a lost tourist.

"You need to see a doctor. Find out why it isn't opening," he said.

"God, that's embarrassing."

He shrugged and turned on the TV. Animal Planet.

"That's what doctors are for," he said. "I can't do much in there. Not if it's all sewn up."

You could say that this was how things started with her mother's landscaper. She was waiting in line to order a double mint-chip cone at McConnel's, wondering what to do about her problem, and there he was, in line right in front of her.

He saw her too. Smiled. These days, men sprouted out of unlikely places, like weeds from invisible cracks in walls.

He pointed to his apartment complex, "I live right over there," he said.

"You live near some very dangerous ice cream," she said and he laughed. That night, she jogged over to his apartment.

"Thank you for such a pleasant distraction," he said, letting her inside.

On Saturday, the boyfriend scratched himself like a flea-ridden dog on her beanbag chair.

"I wonder if we will ever try that again. I'm beginning to worry," he said.

She closed her eyes, aware of her marvelous vagina.

"Don't worry," she said. She felt tired and happy. Sloppy and carefree. When she went to kiss him, his lips felt slippery, like a snail's road home.

HE OWNED BIRDS

HE owned birds. "Always have," he said. The game was not being too frightened to kiss him. He moved the tip of his nose to the tip of her nose, it prolonged the moment of beforeness. She wanted lots of that, lots of quiet staring before the other things happened.

While young and slanted, she wanted a man's slow, steady mouth. Maybe later, kissing would become slushy like Spring snow. But for now, she had the pluck to ask for slowness.

"Kisses come in clusters," he said. "Clusters are nice," she said.

Her mom had squarish shoulders and they were getting manly. Without breasts her mother looked like an empty picture frame.

The shutters on his eyelids opened and she kissed his mouth. She had strength in her lips. She was slim and he liked that, would stay slim forever. Men liked to barely see a woman.

Her lips felt like wrists, or legs. They could do anything. They could change the course of what was going to happen to her.

LETTER FROM AN OLD LOVER

ONE regular morning, you receive a letter. From an old lover. "Hello," it says. "Are you well?"

It's been twenty years. He wants you to know he's become a composer and a concert pianist. His wife an opera singer. "We're performing at the Great American Music Hall next Saturday," he wrote. "We hope you'll come."

When you loved him, he showed no interest in music. He never even allowed you to play music in your car when you tried—*so long ago*—to share your love of Bach. He covered his ears.

And so you wrestle with this in your mind which has lately become a washing machine, turning everything inside of you inside out.

The one who hated dogs became a veterinarian.

The insecure one a well-known actor.

You sit in your cubicle trying to accept your dumbness while co-workers, swimming toward the coffee maker, try not to trip on your legs.

You can't stop wondering about the only one you loved. The one who swore he would never be able to love you back.

BEAUTIFUL REALTORS

You tell yourself: you're going to be fine, because of these realtors flitting around like crows. You and the TV are a team, the last outdated objects to go: dusty, obsolete. Outside, there is a sizzle in the air, as if the sky has an urge to do something. What a nice life you and the ex made, buying this house in a difficult city when you loved each other. How the two of you worked the system until the system worked you back. Even during the best of years, you were too common for this living room's parquet floors, picture window facing the sea. You with moth holes in every sweater. "Someone will snap this up in a second," Candy says. You sigh and pretend you are floating in outer space. *Where to next, Major Tom? Does anyone really belong here on Planet Earth?*

Floating like a dead star in the living room while the beautiful realtors take one last peck through the place you once nested in. There is something reality-show sad about their perky, morning-faces. "Such loving details all over this house," Candy says with the world's most fertile smile.

INFESTATION

THERE was a large cockroach living in my heart, clinking its tender little legs, plotting escape. People's hearts are heavy with bugs they won't admit. Mine remembered everything—the early days of my marriage, dreams of growing old while holding fingers. Driving to Monterey, after his affair, I told my husband about the cockroach. "Smart, but not very optimistic," I said.

There's something about driving to a beautiful place, not looking directly at each other, watching the highway. He said, "I understand. There's a cockroach inside me too."

That night, I felt the tiniest part of me scurrying out, eager to be seen. His sudden disclosure had made my head spin. Under the motel sign, I heard two hearts chirping. We made love for the first time in years, the angels trying to bring us back to each other—as if we recognized a friend in the dark.

BACK AT HOME

BACK at home with the animals, I hear the rat's wheel turning, screeching like a cable car. It must be night. If it is night, then the lights are off. The cats see everything, but the dog is cautious. In the blackout, I hear the quickening sound of little feet, tapping out something that sounds like rice falling. The beat slows and then quickens again. I feel the walls, cool barriers between our rooms. It is still our house, for sure. The pungent smell of all the animals tells me that. There's even a taste in the air, someone cooking the memory of love.

ACKNOWLEDGMENTS

Grateful acknowledgment is made to the following publications in which these stories or earlier versions previously appeared:

"A Detached Kind of Imaginary Cruelty" from the collection *Cellulose Pajamas* (Blue Light Press, 2016)

"Saab Story" *Midway Journal*

"Beautiful Realtors" *Funicular Magazine*

"Cured" *Connotation Press*

"Mood Ring" *KYSO Flash*

"Under Blacklight," "Prescription," and "Bus Vibrations" from the collection *Damn Sure Right* (Press 53, 2011)

"The Rescue" *Milk Candy Review*

"Bike Mechanic" *Spelk*

"The Big Sleep" *Electric Literature*

ABOUT THE AUTHOR

Meg Pokrass is the author of five previous flash fiction collections. Her work has been anthologized in two Norton anthologies including *New Micro* (W.W. Norton & Co., 2018), *Best Small Fictions, 2018* and *2019*, the *Wigleaf Top 50*, and has appeared in 350 literary magazines both online and in print. She currently serves as Flash Challenge Editor at *Mslexia Magazine*, Festival Curator for Flash Fiction Festival, U.K. (Bristol) Co-Editor of *Best Microfiction*, and Founding/Managing Editor of *New Flash Fiction Review*. Her website is megpokrass.com

AUTHOR PHOTO BY MIRIAM BERKELEY

112 Harvard Ave #65
Claremont, CA 91711 USA

pelekinesis@gmail.com
www.pelekinesis.com
Pelekinesis titles are available through Small
Press Distribution, Baker & Taylor, Ingram,
Bertrams, and directly from the publisher's
website.